CONNECTICUT HUSKIES

BY MARTY GITLIN

Published by ABDO Publishing Company, PO Box 398166, Minneapolis, MN 55439.

Printed in the United States of America,
North Mankato, Minnesota
102011
012012

 THIS BOOK CONTAINS AT LEAST 10% RECYCLED MATERIALS.

Editor: Chrös McDougall
Copy Editor: Anna Comstock
Series design and cover production: Craig Hinton
Interior production: Kelsey Oseid

Photo Credits: Ed Reinke/AP Images, cover; Rich Clarkson/NCAA Photos/AP Images, 1; Eric Gay/AP Images, 4, 9, 24, 40; Duncan Williams/Cal Sports Media/AP images, 6, 12; Ryan McKee/NCAA Photos/AP Images, 10, 43 (bottom right); Wil Blanche/Sports Illustrated/Getty Images, 14, 43 (top); Michael Conroy/AP Images, 19, 42 (top); Suzanne Vlamis/AP Images, 20; John Lent/AP Images, 23; Susan Ragan/AP Images, 26, 42 (bottom left); Gerald Herbert/AP Images, 29; Doug Pensinger/AL/Getty Images, 30; Al Bello/Allsport/Getty Images, 33, 42 (bottom right); Chris O'Meara/AP Images, 34; Brett Wilhelm/NCAA Photos/AP Images, 36, 43 (bottom left); Wily Low/AP images, 39; Bob Child/AP Images, 44

Design elements: Matthew Brown/iStockphoto

Library of Congress Cataloging-in-Publication Data
Gitlin, Marty.
Connecticut Huskies / by Marty Gitlin.
p. cm. -- (Inside college basketball)
Includes index.
ISBN 978-1-61783-280-2
1. Connecticut Huskies (Basketball team)--History--Juvenile literature. 2. University of Connecticut--Basketball--History--Juvenile literature. I. Title.
GV885.43.U44G58 2012
796.323'630974643--dc23

2011039992

TABLE OF CONTENTS

The Huskies' Jeremy Lamb goes up for a dunk to begin the second half of the 2011 NCAA Tournament championship game.

1

FLYING HIGH

ANGER FILLED THE CONNECTICUT LOCKER ROOM. IT WAS HALFTIME AT THE 2011 NATIONAL COLLEGIATE ATHLETIC ASSOCIATION (NCAA) TOURNAMENT CHAMPIONSHIP GAME. THE HUSKIES TRAILED THE UNDERDOG BUTLER BULLDOGS 22–19. THE CONNECTICUT PLAYERS WERE MAD AND EMBARRASSED. AND COACH JIM CALHOUN WAS FURIOUS. AFTER ALL, THE TEAM WAS PLAYING POORLY IN FRONT OF 70,000 FANS IN HOUSTON, TEXAS. MILLIONS MORE WERE WATCHING ON TELEVISION ALL ACROSS THE COUNTRY.

Star guard Kemba Walker shouted at his teammates, "Let's do this together!" The players knew they could perform better. They needed to play better defense. They needed to play better offense. And they needed to play with greater intensity.

They did all of that in the second half. The Huskies fell behind by six points. But then they took over. Walker hit a jump shot. Freshman guard Jeremy Lamb nailed a

Jeremy Lamb helped the Huskies win the 2011 Big East Tournament and qualify for the NCAA Tournament.

three-pointer. Center Alex Oriakhi made a layup. Lamb slammed in a dunk and launched another one through the hoop.

Meanwhile, the defense held strong. The Huskies limited the Bulldogs to just one basket during a 13-minute stretch. By the time Butler hit another one, Connecticut led by 13 points. It was all over but the celebration.

And boy did they celebrate. Calhoun hugged everyone in sight. Forward Roscoe Smith blurted out three words: "Joy, joy, happiness." And Walker bragged, "We shocked the world. We were destined."

The 68-year-old Calhoun was more philosophical. He had coached many Huskies teams during his long career. But he knew this team was exceptional; it was more than just talented players. "I've been fortunate enough to have some great teams at UConn," he said. "Very honestly, this group to me will always be incredibly special. . . . I needed this team. Very rarely does a coach say that. . . . Everybody involved, they truly were brothers."

The Huskies were not performing like brothers the year before, in 2009–10. They failed to qualify for the NCAA Tournament for only the second time in nine years. But the 2010–11 season started with great promise. Connecticut won the EA Sports Maui Invitational, a tournament in Hawaii, beating the tough Michigan State Spartans and the Kentucky Wildcats in the process. The Huskies continued to win until they had sprinted out to a 10–0 record. They then won seven of their next nine games.

Connecticut began to struggle as the NCAA Tournament approached, though.

ONE GREAT COACH

Connecticut coach Jim Calhoun is one of the most successful college basketball coaches of all time. He spent 14 years coaching at Northeastern before taking over the Huskies. He led the smaller school to six winning seasons and five NCAA Tournament berths in his last seven years.

Calhoun was just warming up. He coached Connecticut to 24 consecutive winning seasons, 17 NCAA Tournament appearances, and three national championships through 2011. His 855 victories through 2011 ranked sixth all-time among all college coaches.

Calhoun's peers respect him. Among them is Syracuse coach Jim Boeheim, who is fifth on that same list. "People don't mention [Calhoun] that much when they talk about great coaches, but he's done more in taking a program from a [small] conference to the top of college basketball than anybody else has ever done at any school. . . . He's done an unbelievable job."

THE OTHER CHAMPION HUSKIES

Since the 1990s, few college basketball teams have had as much success as the Connecticut Huskies. One of the teams that has had more success is the "other" Connecticut Huskies. The Connecticut women's basketball team, that is. The Connecticut women have won seven NCAA championships from 1995 through 2011. They even won 90 straight games from 2008 to 2010. That is as an all-time NCAA record for a men's or women's team.

The Huskies won only four of their final 11 regular-season games. That left them with a 9–9 record in the Big East Conference.

The players knew something would have to change. The Huskies were still ranked 21st in the nation. But they realized they would have to perform well in the Big East Tournament in order to get a high seed in the NCAA Tournament. And that is exactly what they did.

The Huskies opened the event with an easy win over DePaul. Then they eliminated Georgetown, Pittsburgh, and Syracuse. Finally they faced Louisville in the championship game. Walker scored 19 points to lead the Huskies to a 69–66 victory. It was Connecticut's fifth win in five days of the tournament. It also earned the team a number-three seed in the NCAA Tournament.

Connecticut entered the NCAA Tournament with an advantage over most teams. Walker stood just 6-foot-1. But he was fearless sneaking inside against players nearly a foot taller to score, pass, and even rebound. Few college basketball players had Walker's talents. Even fewer had his ability to take over a game.

Connecticut guard Kemba Walker leaps toward the basket during the 2011 NCAA Tournament final.

Walker averaged 23.5 points per game. That was more than twice as many points as any other player on the team. He also led Connecticut in steals, assists, and free-throw percentage. He was one huge reason why the Huskies were ready when the NCAA Tournament rolled around.

Some people wondered if the Huskies players would be tired after their Big East Tournament victory. But they proved they were not with an 81–52 first-round win over Bucknell. Walker then exploded for a combined 69 points in back-to-back victories over Cincinnati and San Diego State. Walker and Lamb combined for 60 of Connecticut's 74 points against San Diego State.

Calhoun spoke highly of the pair after the victory. He was especially proud that, although they dominated the scoring, they still played team

The Connecticut Huskies hold the NCAA championship trophy after defeating Butler in the 2011 final.

basketball. "Kemba and Jeremy, they're old-fashioned kids, which gives you pleasure, because you aren't coaching egos," Calhoun said.

The Huskies were tested by Arizona in the Elite Eight. Guard Shabazz Napier hit a three-pointer to give Connecticut a nine-point lead midway through the second half. But the Wildcats roared back. Three minutes later, the Huskies were behind. The Huskies came back to take a seven-point lead. But the lead was cut to 65–63 with just one minute left.

The drama soon reached a fever pitch. Wildcats forward Jamelle Horne launched a three-pointer with four seconds left. If it dropped through the net, the Huskies would be done. But it bounced off the rim. Connecticut was in the Final Four. And Lamb let out a big sigh of relief.

ONWARD AND UPWARD

Most basketball experts could not predict where Huskies star guard Kemba Walker would be selected in the 2011 National Basketball Association (NBA) Draft. They knew about his great talent. But they were concerned that his comparatively small stature of 6-foot-1 would scare away teams. It did worry some teams. But it did not prevent the Charlotte Bobcats from snagging Walker with the ninth overall pick.

"I thought [the Horne shot] was definitely going in," he said. "When he missed it I looked at the clock and saw zero-zero, and I just went 'Whooooo.' It's the best feeling I ever had."

The feeling was about to get better. The national semifinal against Kentucky followed the same pattern. Connecticut raced out to a 10-point halftime lead. But Kentucky clawed back to take the lead five minutes into the second half. The game continued to go back and forth. Layups by Napier and Walker put the Huskies ahead 54–48 with 2 minutes, 28 seconds remaining. Connecticut did not score another point until only one second remained. But behind a strong defense, the Huskies held on to win 56–55.

"The guys decided they didn't want to go home; this is too much fun," Calhoun said.

And that was not unusual at Connecticut. The Huskies had been having fun for years by winning championships.

Connecticut's colors have been blue and white since the 1890s, when it was still Connecticut Agricultural College.

2

THE HUSKIES ARE BORN

THE YEAR WAS 1901. ONLY 10 YEARS AFTER JAMES NAISMITH HUNG UP A PEACH BASKET AND INVENTED BASKETBALL, ONE OF THE MOST STORIED COLLEGE BASKETBALL PROGRAMS WAS BORN.

Connecticut Agricultural College would not be known as the University of Connecticut for decades. Its men's basketball team—then known as the Aggies—played one game that year. It was a 17–12 win over Windham High School. The Aggies had no coach for that game. In fact, they had no coach until 1915.

The team's first taste of consistent success arrived when Sumner A. Dole took over the program in 1923. The Aggies won 39 of their 64 games during his four and a half seasons as coach. But the coaching carousel continued. The first one to stay a while was Don White. He took over in 1936 and guided the team—now called the Huskies—to eight consecutive winning seasons.

Coach Hugh Greer led the Huskies to seven NCAA Tournament appearances from 1946 to 1962.

A new era began with the hiring of Hugh Greer five days before Christmas in 1946. The Huskies split his first two games. Then they won 12 straight. It was a sign of good things to come. Greer stayed in charge until midway through the 1962–63 season. He ended his time as the most successful coach in team history to that point.

It helped that Greer arrived when the Huskies boasted one of the premier players in the country. A burly 6-foot-5 center named Walt Dropo averaged 21 points per game in 1945–46. He averaged 19.7 points per game the following year.

But Greer continued to lead the team to victory well after Dropo was gone. He guided the Huskies to Yankee Conference titles in 1948 and 1949. And the Huskies won the conference title every year from 1951 to 1960. "He was a gentleman, a very hard worker, intelligent, very popular, and so very helpful to others," said Nick Rodis, who served as Greer's assistant for eight seasons.

The blossoming of the Connecticut program occurred at an ideal time. The NCAA Tournament began in 1939. That was one year after the National Invitation Tournament (NIT) launched. The Huskies quickly became an annual participant in one or the other. But they could not yet compete against the top programs in the nation. They only won one of their nine NCAA Tournament games under Greer.

Greer achieved his greatest triumph during the winter of 1954. Fans had been waiting all season for a clash against the Holy Cross Crusaders. The Crusaders had beaten Connecticut in 1952 and 1953. Both teams were in top form in 1953–54. The Huskies entered the showdown with a 20–2 record. Holy Cross was a near perfect 22–1. And the Crusaders entered with a 47-game home winning streak.

But the Huskies quickly put that winning streak in jeopardy. The second half was quite dramatic. Huskies star center Art Quimby scored seven straight points down the stretch. Then he tallied another basket to give his team a 76–75 lead with 57 seconds left. However, a steal and basket gave Holy Cross the lead with 14 seconds remaining.

Greer called timeout. He set up a play for forward Worthy Patterson. "Someone came right at me when I got the ball, and I just went around him and laid it up," Patterson said. "And when it went

WORTHY PATTERSON

Worthy Patterson was a Huskies standout during the early 1950s. He hoped to stick with the NBA's Boston Celtics after finishing his college career. But he was the last player cut from the team in training camp. Patterson did compete very briefly for the St. Louis Hawks. That team featured future Basketball Hall of Fame players Bob Pettit and Cliff Hagan. But Patterson got into only four games and scored just seven points.

through the net, it was like, 'Yes'—and the place went wild." The Huskies had clinched a huge victory.

The NCAA Tournament determines the official national champion of college basketball. However, the NIT was once considered the more prestigious postseason tournament. That was especially true for East Coast teams. After all, the NIT was held at the glamorous Madison Square Garden in New York City.

The Huskies only landed one NIT berth during the 1950s era, and they lost in the first round. They did not have much more success in the NCAA Tournament either. Connecticut lost in its opening game six times during Greer's 12 full seasons from 1947–48 to 1961–62. There was one exception in 1956. The Huskies defeated the Manhattan Jaspers for their first tournament win. Then they nearly upset the powerful Temple Owls in the Sweet 16, but they came up just short.

The Huskies were in the midst of another strong regular season in 1962–63 when tragedy struck. Greer suffered a heart attack while playing handball. He died in January 1963.

New coach Fred Shabel finally broke the trend of postseason failure in 1964. The Huskies beat Temple in the first round of the NCAA Tournament. Many fans were satisfied with the win. They did not expect much more. After all, the Huskies had to face the heavily favored Princeton Tigers in the second round. Even Princeton coach Bill van Breda Kolff figured his team would crush Connecticut. So he did not even bother watching the Huskies' win over Temple. When asked why he did not scout the Connecticut team, he replied that a team could not be very good if it only scored about 50 points a game.

The Huskies set out to prove him wrong. They bolted to an early lead. However, Princeton came back to tie the game at 50–50 with 30 seconds remaining. Connecticut senior guard Dom Perno was not a great shooter. But he was good enough to sink two late foul shots to give his team the

THREE-SPORT STAR

Walt Dropo was arguably the greatest all-around athlete in University of Connecticut history. After starring in baseball, basketball, and football in college, Dropo was drafted to play professional basketball and football. However, he ended up as an All-Star in Major League Baseball.

Dropo exploded onto the scene with the Boston Red Sox in 1950. He drove in 144 runs and earned Rookie of the Year honors. Two years later he set a record that still stood in 2011 by collecting a hit in 12 consecutive trips to the plate. Dropo also served as an army combat engineer for three years during World War II.

"He was a giant of a man and very proud of his family and heritage," Connecticut athletic department spokesperson Dee Rowe said after Dropo died in 2010. "When he walked into a room, he had this great presence. You knew he was there and he just captured everyone."

MORE ABOUT WES

Huskies star Wes Bialosuknia produced some of the most explosive games in school history. He scored 40 points in a win against Boston College as a sophomore. And he tallied a school-record 50 points in another victory against Maine. The NBA's St. Louis Hawks drafted Bialosuknia in 1967. However, he did not sign because they could not ensure he would make the roster. Instead he hooked up with Oakland of the upstart American Basketball Association. There he played 70 games during the 1967–68 season and averaged 8.7 points per game.

lead. Perno then stole the ball from Princeton star Bill Bradley to clinch the victory.

The win was made even sweeter because Connecticut had scored just 52 points. Van Breda Kolff never would have believed that would be enough to beat his team. But Shabel was happy the game ended when it did.

"I just remember how thankful I was the clock had run out," Shabel said. "We had had the lead and control most of the game, but they were finishing strong. Had the game lasted much longer, I did not like our chances."

The powerful Duke Blue Devils clobbered the Huskies with a Final Four berth on the line, but Connecticut fans were still thrilled. Their team had achieved the longest postseason run in school history.

The winning ways continued into the 1964–65 season. Connecticut tied its best regular-season finish ever with a 23–3 record. That included a 15-game winning streak to end the season. The Huskies also featured one of the top 1–2 punches in college basketball in sophomore guard

Huskies fans always show up to the game ready to cheer on their team.

Wes Bialosuknia and senior center Toby Kimball. The pair had combined to score 41.1 points per game. And Kimball averaged a remarkable 21 rebounds per game.

"I think Toby is the greatest player in UConn history," Bialosuknia said years later. "He was the whole package, a great rebounder, leader, and person."

The good times did not last for the Huskies. Connecticut fans were growing weary of the early postseason exits. However, just getting to the postseason would be a treat for the next several seasons.

Connecticut lost to the South Carolina Gamecocks 71–61 in the first round of the 1975 NIT.

3

DRY SPELL

THE HUSKIES' FUTURE LOOKED BRIGHT WHEN THEY NEARLY REACHED THE 1964 FINAL FOUR. FEW COULD HAVE IMAGINED THEN THAT THE TEAM WOULD WIN JUST ONE MORE NCAA TOURNAMENT GAME OVER THE NEXT 26 YEARS.

Fred Shabel had been the Huskies' coach in 1964. But he left the program after just four years following the 1966–67 season. Shabel wanted to be an athletic director. So when the University of Pennsylvania offered him that position, he jumped at the opportunity. During his four years at Connecticut, Shabel guided the Huskies to four Yankee Conference titles and three NCAA Tournament berths. Connecticut did not reach another NCAA Tournament for nine years.

Burr Carlson replaced Shabel as coach. He had starred as a player for Connecticut during the early 1950s. But he struggled in his role as the new coach. The Huskies dropped to 11–13 during his first season, in 1967–68. They then

GOOD PLAYER, GREAT COACH

Many basketball fans do not know that Tom Penders was a talented guard for the Huskies during the mid-1960s. But they do know that he was one of the top coaches in the history of college basketball. Penders began his coaching career at Tufts University in 1971. He coached six other teams, but he was best known for leading the University of Texas to eight NCAA Tournament appearances in 10 years. Penders retired in 2010 with 648 victories. He was 24th on the all-time list of Division I college coaches in wins when he called it quits.

dropped to 5–19 the following year. It was their worst record in 49 years.

A team that had prided itself on defense could not stop opponents under Carlson. The Huskies lost their first 10 games of the 1968–69 season. They surrendered nearly 90 points per game in the process. Carlson quit after two years. The school turned to Massachusetts high school coaching legend Dee Rowe as his replacement. Rowe had turned Worcester Academy into a dynasty.

Rowe came to Connecticut promising to restore the Huskies' winning tradition begun by Hugh Greer more than two decades earlier. But Rowe did not get off to a good start. After going 14–9 during his first season, Rowe's Huskies then suffered through two losing seasons. But the Huskies began to win in 1973. They had five straight winning seasons under Rowe. They made the NIT in 1974 and 1975, reaching the quarterfinals in 1974. And they even returned to the NCAA Tournament in 1976.

The Huskies trailed Hofstra by 15 points in the first round. But they stormed back to force overtime. The game was tied at 78–78 when junior guard Joey Whelton nailed a shot to give Connecticut the victory.

Connecticut guard/forward Tony Hanson attempts to block a shot during the 1974 NIT.

Connecticut lost to the undefeated Rutgers Scarlet Knights in the second round. But Rowe had indeed brought the program back to a high standing. One of the ways he did it was by recruiting star players such as guard/forward Tony Hanson. Hanson averaged 26 points and 10.5 rebounds per game during his senior year in 1976–77. And he had a place in his heart for Rowe.

"Dee Rowe is a very special man," Hanson said. "He's like a godfather to me, to all of us really. Obviously his focus was on the court, but a lot of his influence was off the court in life and academics. He's a good man."

Jonathan the Husky has been the University of Connecticut's mascot since 1965.

Rowe did not stay around to build upon his success, though. Coaching burned him out, and he developed medical problems. So he resigned after the 1976–77 season to spend more time with his family.

Changes were not just in store for Rowe. They were in store for the entire basketball program. Former Huskies star Dom Perno took over as coach in 1977–78. He led the team to an Eastern College Athletic Conference title and NCAA Tournament berth in 1979. But the most significant move came from athletic director John Toner. He helped form a new league for his school to join.

The Big East Conference was launched in 1979. It would blossom into one of the finest athletic conferences in the country. Connecticut still played in the conference in 2011. But the Big East competition was far stronger than what the 1979 Huskies were used to. They could no longer dominate a field of weaker conference opponents. The Huskies were good enough to qualify for the NIT in 1980, 1981, and 1982. However, they were merely 18–16 in Big East competition during those three years.

CONNECTICUT COLLAPSE

The Huskies generally dominated non-conference opponents soon after the Big East was formed. But their record plummeted when they began playing conference foes. The most dramatic example occurred during the 1983–84 season. They boasted an 8–3 record in non-conference games that season. But in the Big East, the Huskies lost 10 of their last 12 games (including the conference tournament).

"We knew if we lacked a total long-term commitment to upgrade, it would be a problem," Perno said. "For example, we loved the Field House [the Huskies' home court] on game nights, but we also knew it had aged and could not compare to other facilities we were competing against. One time we had to divert a recruit from seeing the Field House due to a leaking roof."

The Huskies also could not match the talent of their Big East competition. They suffered through losing seasons every year from 1982–83 to 1985–86 under Perno. They sported a terrible 19–45 record against league opponents during that stretch. Angry fans called for Perno to resign, which he did in 1986.

The Huskies then went in search of a coach who could win in the Big East and take the team to new heights in the NCAA Tournament. They found that man in Jim Calhoun.

Coach Jim Calhoun has led the Huskies to three NCAA championships as of 2011.

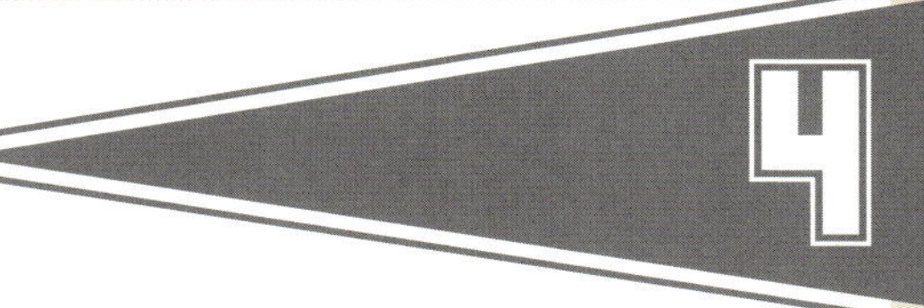

SOARING TO THE TOP

IT WAS DECEMBER 28, 1985. CONNECTICUT ATHLETIC DIRECTOR JOHN TONER WAS WATCHING HIS TEAM PLAY THE NORTHEASTERN HUSKIES IN AN EARLY-SEASON TOURNAMENT. CONNECTICUT WAS SUPPOSED TO WIN. BUT NORTHEASTERN WON BY 17 POINTS TO EARN THE CHAMPIONSHIP.

Toner was impressed with the way Northeastern performed. "I saw how intently the Northeastern players listened to their coach, how hard they played, and what good shape they were in at the end of the game," he said.

Toner was also captivated with Northeastern coach Jim Calhoun. He remembered that Northeastern game when Dom Perno resigned as Connecticut's coach after that season. So Toner asked Calhoun to take over the Huskies. Former coach Dee Rowe convinced Calhoun to accept the job. Toner was thrilled, because there was something else he knew about Calhoun.

"With Northeastern, Calhoun often could only recruit second- or third-level players," he said, "but he used excellent coaching and better conditioning to get the most out of them."

At a bigger school like Connecticut, Calhoun would be able to recruit top-level players. And that is what he did. Calhoun soon attracted some of the top high school players in the country. But it took some time for him to transform the Huskies into title contenders. In fact, they finished only 9–19 in Calhoun's first season, 1986–87. That was their worst season since 1971–72. But the Huskies did not suffer another losing season again through 2011.

Connecticut blossomed into one of the premier teams in college basketball in 1990 when it steamrolled to the brink of the Final Four. Only the Duke Blue Devils stood in the Huskies' way. But the Huskies lost in the Elite Eight in one of the most famous plays in NCAA Tournament history. Connecticut led 78–77 with the final seconds of overtime ticking away. But Blue Devils forward Christian Laettner buried a 14-foot jumper with one second remaining to give his team the victory.

SIZZLING STREAK

The 1995–96 Huskies were upset in the NCAA Tournament, but they did set a school record with an amazing 23-game winning streak. The team went nearly three months without tasting defeat. The incredible stretch began with an 86–52 trouncing of Indiana, and it ended with a 77–65 loss to Georgetown.

Connecticut's Dan Cyrulik, *left*, and Chris Smith, *right*, celebrate winning the 1990 Big East Tournament.

Calhoun continued to guide Connecticut into the NCAA Tournament in the following years. He recruited some future NBA standouts during that period.

Among those players were guard Ray Allen and forwards Donyell Marshall and Richard "Rip" Hamilton. Allen and Marshall combined to

Huskies guard Ray Allen was a consensus All-American during the 1995–96 season.

score 37 points per game during the 1993–94 season. Some people thought that might be the year the Huskies took the next step to the Final Four. They finished the regular season ranked second in the nation. The Huskies then rolled easily to the Sweet 16. There, Connecticut sprinted to a 10-point lead against the underdog Florida Gators.

However, the Huskies fell short of the Elite Eight. They collapsed in the second half and lost in overtime. Allen scored just two points in the game. And Huskies fans began to wonder if they would ever experience a championship.

They continued to wonder through most of the 1990s. The Huskies again surged to the brink of a Final Four berth in 1995. But again they lost, this time to top-ranked University of California, Los Angeles (UCLA). The Huskies earned a ranking of third in the country in 1996. Yet the upstart Mississippi State Bulldogs stunned them in the Sweet 16.

A New York newspaper mocked Connecticut's inability to reach the Final Four. It changed the common "UConn" reference to "UCan't." The reference was insulting, but the Huskies knew there was only one way to shed the nickname. They did not do that in 1998, though. The Huskies took an 11-game winning streak into the Elite Eight, but there the top-ranked North Carolina Tar Heels outclassed them.

FROM CONNECTICUT TO NBA HOTSHOT

Many top-tier college basketball players struggle to be as dominant in the NBA. But that was not the case with guard Ray Allen. He proved to be even greater in the NBA than he was at Connecticut. The 6-foot-5 guard scored more than 20 points per game every year from 1999–2000 to 2006–07. He was named to the All-Star team 10 times through 2010–11. His quick release of the ball and deadly accuracy made him one of the top three-point shooters in the history of the sport. He set the NBA record for most three-pointers made in a career in 2011.

The 1998–99 season started out in a familiar pattern. Hamilton led the way with 22 points per game. Sophomore point guard Khalid El-Amin guided the offense. And behind Hamilton and El-Amin, the Huskies were ranked third heading into the NCAA Tournament. But this time they were not to be denied. They sealed a Final Four berth with a

"RIPPING" IT UP

Richard "Rip" Hamilton was one of the finest players in Connecticut history. He emerged as a star in the NBA as well. He proved to be among the most consistently productive shooters in the league. Hamilton spent three years with the Washington Wizards before blossoming with the Detroit Pistons. He scored between 17 and 20 points per game every year from 1999–2000 to 2009–10. He also played a huge role in the Pistons' run to the NBA title in 2004 and appeared in three All-Star Games through 2011.

67–62 victory over Gonzaga. Years of frustration had finally ended.

The Huskies still had work to do, though. And they had to do it in unfamiliar territory. The Final Four games had become some of the biggest sporting events of the year in the United States. More than 40,000 fans packed the arena in St. Petersburg, Florida. But the Huskies were not intimidated.

Connecticut's defense held Ohio State in check during the semifinal game. Ohio State shot just 24 percent in the second half. Meanwhile, Hamilton continued to roll with 24 points. The result was a 64–58 victory and a title-game berth against top-ranked Duke.

Many people considered Duke to be one of the finest teams in the history of college basketball. The Huskies' players tuned in to a TV preview of the championship game the night before the competition. They were stunned and angered to see that Duke fans had already produced t-shirts and balloons that hailed the Blue Devils as champions.

"We're watching this like, are you serious?" said senior Rashamel Jones. "We haven't even played the game yet, and they've got T-shirts

Connecticut guard Richard "Rip" Hamilton dribbles the ball up the court during a 1997 game against Seton Hall.

and balloons made up. That's a slap in our face. You know what, tomorrow we're [going to] beat Duke."

The basketball world held its breath, waiting to find out if Jones and the Huskies could indeed overcome the powerful Blue Devils.

Ricky Moore grabs the ball after Duke's Trajan Langdon is called for traveling in the 1999 NCAA championship game.

5

MORE STARS, MORE TITLES

JIM CALHOUN DEVISED A PLAN AS HE PREPARED HIS EAGER HUSKIES FOR THEIR FIRST NATIONAL TITLE GAME. HE DECIDED TO RUN A FAST-PACED OFFENSE AND DOUBLE-TEAM DUKE STAR CENTER ELTON BRAND. THE STRATEGY WORKED TO PERFECTION. BRAND WAS FRUSTRATED BECAUSE HE NEVER KNEW WHICH PLAYERS WERE COMING OVER TO GUARD HIM.

The Huskies led 75–74 with 15 seconds remaining in the game. Duke senior Trajan Langdon had the ball. Blue Devils coach Mike Krzyzewski told Langdon to take Connecticut guard Ricky Moore to the basket for the winning shot. But Moore had other ideas.

"I loved that," Moore said. "Him against me. All I had to do was get one stop. I started smiling because I knew he wasn't going to score that basket."

And he was right. Moore did not let Langdon break free. Langdon dribbled one way and then the other before the

Connecticut guard Ben Gordon was the 2004 Big East Tournament's Most Outstanding Performer.

referee called him for traveling. Soon the game was over. The Huskies had won their first NCAA title. Junior guard Richard "Rip" Hamilton was named the tournament's Most Outstanding Player.

Former Connecticut coach Dee Rowe felt proud that he had convinced Calhoun to accept the job 13 years earlier. "Jim Calhoun has taken UConn basketball to the top of the mountain, to a place never before even dreamed of," he said. "He has truly performed a miracle." There would be more miracles to come.

The Huskies had finally learned how to win. Calhoun had given the school a reputation of basketball greatness. Add in his ability to recruit the best high school players in the nation, and the Connecticut basketball program had a deadly combination.

The 1999 championship helped Calhoun attract more players destined for NBA stardom. Perhaps the best of all were forward Caron Butler, guard Ben Gordon, and center Emeka Okafor. All three played within four years of that championship season.

Butler played for the Huskies from 2000–2001 to 2001–02. He averaged 20 points per game in 2001–02. But he did not experience an NCAA title. That thrill belonged to Gordon and Okafor. Gordon scored 17 points per game for the Huskies during his three-year career. And Okafor averaged 14 points and 11 rebounds per game while providing stifling defense.

ONE WAY TO REMEMBER

Huskies forward Shamon Tooles wanted his teammates to be inspired for the 2003–04 season. So after a 2003 loss to Texas in the Sweet 16, he wrote down the score of that game on his sneaker. He believed the words "Texas 82, Connecticut 78" would be a constant reminder the next year of how painful the defeat was. It seemed to work. The Huskies played the 2004 NCAA Tournament like they did not want to experience another heartbreaking loss. And they won the national championship.

Butler, Gordon, and Okafor helped Connecticut reach the Elite Eight in 2002. Gordon and Okafor got the Huskies back to the Sweet 16 in 2003. And they would do even better in 2004. Gordon and Okafor led the Huskies to a Big East Tournament championship. The team carried its momentum into the NCAA Tournament. The Huskies won their first four games by an average of 18 points to reach the Final Four.

Fate always seemed to place Duke in the way. The 2004 season was no exception. The Blue Devils awaited the Huskies in the semifinals. The rematch of the 1999 NCAA title game appeared to be going against the Huskies. Duke built a 73–64 lead with less than five minutes left. But Gordon and Okafor led a stirring comeback. Okafor snagged away a rebound from Duke star Luol Deng. He then put the ball in the basket to give Connecticut a 76–75 lead with 26 seconds left. The Huskies stopped the Blue Devils in six straight possessions down the stretch to win.

The comeback happened so quickly that Okafor could not remember how it happened when it was over. "I just know we [finally] took the lead and, dang, the next thing you know, the game was over and we were all hopping around, jumping and celebrating," he said.

The title-game triumph against the Georgia Tech Yellow Jackets was much easier. The Huskies sprinted to a 60–35 lead and coasted the rest

RUDY GAY IN THE NBA

Rudy Gay was known as a steady player with the Connecticut Huskies. That reputation did not change when he turned pro. The Houston Rockets selected Gay in the 2006 NBA Draft, but they immediately traded him to the Memphis Grizzlies. After his first year, he blossomed into one of the most productive and consistent players in the league. Gay averaged between 18.9 and 20.1 points per game and shot between 45 and 47 percent from the field in each of the next four seasons.

Huskies center Emeka Okafor, *left*, was named the 2004 National Defensive Player of the Year.

of the way. The victory avenged a lopsided regular-season loss to the Yellow Jackets.

The revolving door of basketball stars continued to turn at Connecticut. Following their second national championship, Calhoun recruited premier players such as forwards Rudy Gay and Charlie Villanueva, center Hasheem Thabeet, and guard Kemba Walker.

But the newest generation of Huskies learned that talent alone could not win titles. The 2006 Huskies were ranked second in the nation. But the unranked George Mason Patriots upset them in the Elite Eight. The 2007 team then lost eight of 10 games at midseason and failed to

Connecticut's Alex Oriakhi celebrates as time expires in the 2011 NCAA championship game.

qualify for the NCAA Tournament. It was the first time in six years that Connecticut missed the tournament. The following year, San Diego State stunned the Huskies in the first round of the 2008 tournament.

Some fans began to worry that Connecticut had begun a downward spiral. But 7-foot-3 center Hasheem Thabeet and Walker had other ideas. Walker was a freshman in 2009. But he scored 23 points in a victory over the Missouri Tigers that sent the Huskies into the Final Four. Teammate A. J. Price exclaimed that he had seen Walker mature into manhood that very day.

"I told Kemba [with 10 minutes left in the game] he's growing up today," Price said. "He grew up. He played like a man among boys. There were times he dominated the game. . . . He played phenomenally today and I couldn't be more happy for him."

The happiness wore off when the Huskies lost to the Michigan State Spartans in the semifinals. But two years later, Walker and his teammates would capture a national title—the third for the Huskies in just 13 years.

There were no more doubters. The Connecticut program had been firmly established as one of the best in the history of college basketball.

WALKER STANDS TALL

Some top college basketball players leave school early if they have an opportunity to play in the NBA. But Kemba Walker was not one of them. Walker received a degree in sociology in August 2011. His work ethic in the classroom matched his work ethic on the court. And according to Huskies academic counselor Felicia Crump, it filtered down to his teammates.

"If he's not on time, he's always early," Crump said of Walker. "He will pull the other guys and say, 'You gotta be here. You gotta get your work done.' So it's been great when he's in study hall working or the first one there or staying late because he has the most aggressive schedule. The younger guys don't know any different, so they just follow suit, which has been amazing, and it's been great for me because other guys are talking about, 'I wanna be on the path that Kemba's on. How do I do that? What do I need to do to do that?'"

TIMELINE

1901

A team known as the Connecticut Agricultural College Aggies plays its first basketball game, defeating Windham High School 17–12.

1915

John Donahue is hired as the first Aggies coach. He concludes the season with a 5–3 record.

1922

The Aggies finish their finest year to date, winning 15 of 19 games under new coach J. W. Tasker. But he leaves during the next season.

1934

The school, now known as Connecticut State College, adopts the Huskies nickname for its sports teams. The school becomes the University of Connecticut in 1939.

1936

Don White begins his tenure as Huskies coach and embarks on eight consecutive winning seasons.

1965

Wes Bialosuknia and Toby Kimball team up for one of the top 1–2 punches in program history, but the Huskies are upset by St. Joseph's 67–61 in the first round of the NCAA Tournament on March 8.

1976

The Huskies defeat Hofstra 80–78 in the first round of the NCAA Tournament on March 13 after several lean years.

1986

Jim Calhoun is hired as new Huskies coach on May 15.

1992

A flood of top recruits begin coming to Connecticut, starting with Donyell Marshall. He is followed by Ray Allen and Richard "Rip" Hamilton.

1999

In the Huskies' first-ever trip to the Final Four, they win the championship with a 77–74 defeat over Duke on March 29.

1946

Hugh Greer takes over as coach of the Huskies. Walt Dropo averages 21 points per game and is recognized as the finest player in team history to that point.

1951

A 22–4 season ends with a loss to St. John's on March 20 in the Huskies' first-ever NCAA Tournament game.

1954

The Huskies win at Holy Cross 78–77 on February 27 in one of the most storied games in team history.

1956

Connecticut wins its first NCAA Tournament game on March 13, beating Manhattan 84–75.

1964

New coach Fred Shabel guides the Huskies into the Elite Eight with a 52–50 win over Princeton on March 14.

2000

Three of the premier players in school history begin to bolster the team. Caron Butler joins in 2000 while Ben Gordon and Emeka Okafor follow in 2001.

2004

Coach Jim Calhoun guides Connecticut to its second NCAA Tournament title in six years with an 82–73 win over Georgia Tech on April 5.

2005

Forward Rudy Gay comes to Connecticut, beginning a new generation for the Huskies. He is followed by Hasheem Thabeet and Kemba Walker.

2007

The Huskies fail to make the NCAA Tournament for the only time between 2002 and 2009.

2011

The Huskies win their third NCAA championship since 1999 with a 53–41 defeat of Butler on April 4.

QUICK STATS

PROGRAM INFO

Connecticut Agricultural School Aggies (1901–32)
Connecticut State College Huskies (1933–38)
University of Connecticut Huskies (1939–)

NCAA TOURNAMENT FINALS
(WINS IN BOLD)

1999, 2004, 2011

OTHER ACHIEVEMENTS

Final Fours: 4
NCAA Tournaments: 29
Big East Tournament titles: 7

KEY PLAYERS
(POSITION(S); YEARS WITH TEAM)

Ray Allen (G; 1993–96)
Wes Bialosuknia (G; 1964–67)
Caron Butler (F; 2000–02)
Walt Dropo (C; 1942–43, 1945–47)
Ben Gordon (G; 2001–04)
Richard "Rip" Hamilton (F; 1996–99)
Tony Hanson (G-F; 1973–77)
Toby Kimball (C; 1962–65)
Donyell Marshall (F; 1991–94)
Emeka Okafor (C; 2001–04)
Worthy Patterson (G; 1951–54)
Art Quimby (C; 1951–55)
Cliff Robinson (F; 1985–89)
Corny Thompson (F; 1978–82)
Kemba Walker (G; 2008–11)

KEY COACHES

Jim Calhoun (1986–): 607–230; 48–14 (NCAA Tournament)
Hugh Greer (1946–63): 287–113; 1–8 (NCAA Tournament)

HOME ARENA

Gampel Pavilion (1990–)

* All statistics through 2010–11 season

QUOTES & ANECDOTES

The Huskies did not qualify for the 1988 NCAA Tournament in Jim Calhoun's second year as coach. But their performance in the NIT did bring them a measure of prestige. They won the event by defeating Ohio State in the final, leading to greater success. The triumph meant little to some Connecticut fans, but it did inspire a student celebration at the Field House. The team also was honored at the state capitol building in Hartford.

"Guys have to sacrifice. Everybody is great coming out of high school. Everybody is the man on their team, the leaders. But when you go to another level, things change. For people to sacrifice their games makes them better people."
—Huskies star guard Kemba Walker on becoming a team player

Wes Bialosuknia boasts the highest scoring average in Huskies history—and no one else has even come close. He tallied 23.6 points per game during his career, which is nearly three points more than Walt Dropo. There is also no comparison between the top rebounders. Art Quimby snagged an incredible 21.5 rebounds per game. Toby Kimball, who played alongside Bialosuknia, is next on the list with 17.9.

GLOSSARY

assist
A pass that leads directly to a made shot.

athletic director
An administrator who oversees the coaches, players, and teams of an institution.

conference
In sports, a group of teams that plays each other each season.

consensus
Unanimous agreement.

draft
A system used by professional sports leagues to select new players in order to spread incoming talent among all teams. The NBA Draft is held each June.

dynasty
A team that maintains its position of power for a long time.

momentum
A continued strong performance based on recent success.

overtime
A period in a basketball game that is played to determine a winner when the four quarters end in a tie.

rebound
To secure the basketball after a missed shot.

recruit
To entice a player to come to a certain school to play on its basketball team. A player being sought after is known as a recruit.

retired
To have officially ended one's career.

roster
The players as a whole on a basketball team.

seed
In basketball, a ranking system used for tournaments. The best teams earn a number-one seed.

upset
A result where the supposedly worse team defeats the supposedly better team.

FOR MORE INFORMATION

FURTHER READING

Calhoun, Jim with Leigh Montville. *Dare to Dream: Connecticut basketball's Remarkable March to the National Championship.* New York: Broadway Books, 1999.

Harrison, Don. *Hoops in Connecticut: The Nutmeg State's Passion for Basketball.* Charleston, SC: History Press, 2011.

Hartford Courant. *Top Dogs: UConn Huskies' 2003–04 Men's Championship Season.* Champaign, IL: Sports Publishing, LLC, 2004.

WEB LINKS

To learn more about the Connecticut Huskies, visit ABDO Publishing Company online at **www.abdopublishing.com.** Web sites about the Huskies are featured on our Book Links page. These links are routinely monitored and updated to provide the most current information available.

PLACES TO VISIT

College Basketball Experience
1401 Grand Blvd.
Kansas City, MO 64106
816-949-7500
www.collegebasketballexperience.com

This museum is open Wednesday through Sunday and features a college basketball hall of fame and a number of interactive exhibits in which kids can test their skills.

Harry A. Gampel Pavilion
2095 Hillside Road
Storrs, CN 06269
860-486-4712
www.uconnhuskies.com/facilities/gampel-pavilion.html

The Huskies have been playing their home games here since 1990. It seats just over 10,000 fans.

Naismith Memorial Basketball Hall of Fame
1000 West Columbus Avenue
Springfield, MA 01104
413-781-6500
www.hoophall.com

This all-encompassing hall of fame and museum features the great players and teams from the history of the NBA and college basketball.

INDEX

ABOUT THE AUTHOR

Marty Gitlin is a freelance writer based in Cleveland, Ohio. He has written more than 45 educational books. Gitlin has won more than 45 awards during his 25 years as a writer, including first place for general excellence from the Associated Press. He lives with his wife and three children.